# RAIN TALK

# RAIN TALK

Mary Serfozo
illustrated by Keiko Narahashi

Aladdin Paperbacks

To Maureen and Judith and sharing

M . S .


For Peter and Micah

K . N.

Aladdin Paperbacks
An imprint of Simon & Schuster
Children's Publishing Division
1230 Avenue of the Americas
New York, NY 10020
Text copyright © 1990 by Mary Serfozo
Illustrations copyright © 1990 by Keiko Narahashi
All rights reserved including the right of reproduction
in whole or in part in any form.
First Aladdin Paperbacks edition, 1993
Printed in Hong Kong
10 9 8 7 6 5 4 3 2
A hardcover edition of Rain Talk is available from
Margaret K. McElderry Books

Library of Congress Cataloging-in-Publication Data
Serfozo, Mary.
Rain talk / Mary Serfozo ; illustrated by Keiko Narahashi.–1st
Aladdin Books ed.
p.     cm.
Summary: A child enjoys a glorious day in the rain, listening to the
varied sounds it makes as it comes down.
ISBN 0-689-71699-0
[1. Rain and rainfall–Fiction.]  I. Narahashi, Keiko, ill.
II. Title.
[PZ7.S482Rai   1993]
[E]–dc20                                                        92-29562

$P$*loomp* go the first fat raindrops,

*Ploomp Ploomp Ploomp*
into the soft summer dust
of a country road.

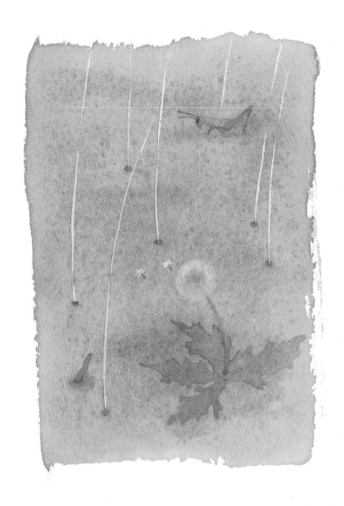

Each little drop digs a dark little hole
and the smell of wet dust tickles my nose.

On the old tin roof of the garden shed
the drops all try to talk at once...
*Ping Ping PingaDing*
*Ping Ping Ping Ping Ping...*

To Mother Duck
that says,
"Time to go for a swim."

Out on the highway
the raindrops bounce high,
and *Whoosh* and *Hiss*
as the cars hurry by.

Headlights are coming on,
reaching out to catch
the silvery slants of rain.

Now all I can hear
is the *Bup Bup Bup Bup*
of rain thumping on my umbrella...

and dropping and dripping all around.

Mother says to come in the house
and the rain tries to come in too...
*Flick...Flick...Flick*ing itself
like pebbles against the windowpanes.

*I*'d rather stay outside.

When I've had my supper and bath
I lie in front of the fire. And now and then
a raindrop slips down the chimney
to *Spit* and *Sizzle* on the logs.

I'm getting very sleepy here.

Tucked into my bed upstairs
I try to stay awake and listen to the
*Drum-a-tum-a-Drum-a-tum-a-Drum-a-tum*
on the roof above my head.

But my eyes…just won't…stay…open.

Tomorrow I may find the rain all gone,
with only a sparkle still caught
in a spiderweb or a flower.

But I'll look first...

for a rainbow!